B

W9-BJB-812

Farm Twins

by Liza Charlesworth

ISBN-13: 978-0-545-25649-0 / ISBN-10: 0-545-25649-6

Illustrated by Anne Kennedy
Designed by Maria Lilja • Colored by Ka-Yeon Kim-Li
Copyright © 2010 by Liza Charlesworth

■SCHOLASTIC

Twin cows say, "MOO, MOO!"

Twin pigs say, "OINK, OINK!"

Twin lambs say, "BAAH, BAAH!"

Twin ducks say, "QUACK, QUACK!"

Twin chicks say, "PEEP, PEEP!"

Twin horses say, "NEIGH, NEIGH!"

Twin girls say, "HELLO, HELLO!"